The
Goblin King

HarperCollins Children's Books is a division of
HarperCollinsPublishers Ltd,
77-85 Fulham Palace Road, Hammersmith, London W6 8JB

Visit us on the web at
www.harpercollins.co.uk

1

SOPHIE AND THE SHADOW WOODS : THE GOBLIN KING

ISBN 978-0-00-741163-4

Printed and bound in England by
Clays Ltd, St Ives plc

Mixed Sources
Product group from well-managed
forests and other controlled sources
www.fsc.org Cert no. SW-COC-001806
© 1996 Forest Stewardship Council
FSC

FSC is a non-profit international organisation established to promote the
responsible management of the world's forests. Products carrying the FSC
label are independently certified to assure consumers that they come
from forests that are managed to meet the social, economic and
ecological needs of present and future generations.

Find out more about HarperCollins and the environment at
www.harpercollins.co.uk/green

Linda Chapman & Lee Weatherly

The
Goblin King

HarperCollins *Children's Books*

To Amany Lily Chapman

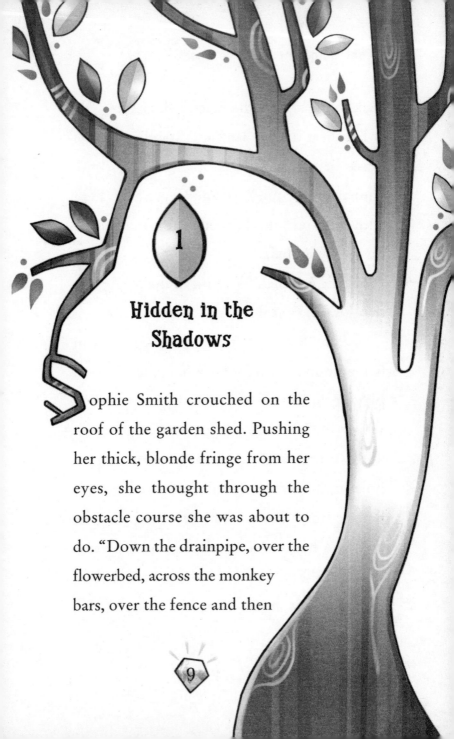

1

Hidden in the Shadows

Sophie Smith crouched on the roof of the garden shed. Pushing her thick, blonde fringe from her eyes, she thought through the obstacle course she was about to do. "Down the drainpipe, over the flowerbed, across the monkey bars, over the fence and then back to the shed," she muttered. Easy!

Her best friend, Sam, was standing on the grass below with a stopwatch. "So, the winner is the quickest one to get back here with the key?" he checked. The wind ruffled his spiky red hair.

Sophie grinned. "You mean the magic key that Dracula's stolen," she corrected him.

She and Sam had found a wooden box in her grandpa's wardrobe when they'd been playing hide-and-seek a few hours earlier. Inside the box was a large iron key, carved with strange and beautiful patterns with a hole in the centre. Sophie had never seen it before, but it looked so interesting that she and Sam had immediately invented a game with it. She planned to put it back before Grandpa got home. For the rest of that

morning, she and Sam had pretended it was a magic key that they had to rescue from Dracula's castle. It had been great fun and, after lunch, the game had turned into a timed obstacle course in the garden.

While some of the girls in her class at school liked to play games about fairies and others liked to giggle about boys, Sophie's favourite things to do were having races, playing on her skateboard and going to tae kwon do classes. She lived in jeans and t-shirts, and though she had long, blonde hair down to her waist, she never put ribbons or bows in it. When she grew up she wanted to be a stuntwoman in films.

Now she looked across the garden, her green eyes narrowing as she got ready. She was determined to be the fastest! "Are you going to time me then, Sam?"

"Yep!" Sam poised his finger above the stopwatch. "On your marks... get set... GO!"

Sophie jumped on to the drainpipe and slid down it as fast as she could. The second her trainers touched the ground, she was off. She sprinted across the grass, her blonde ponytail bouncing up and down.

Leaping over the flowerbed, she ran to the climbing frame. As she reached the top, she flung herself on to the monkey bars and wriggled her way across, swinging her body from side to side. On the platform on the other side she hesitated, but decided not to bother with the ladder. Instead she jumped, feeling a moment of scary weightlessness before she landed. She bounced to her feet and was off again. Excitement buzzed through

her as she charged to the end of the garden
and scrambled over the fence.

There was a wood on the other side – a
thick, deep forest called Shadow Woods with
tall trees that shut out the light. No one ever

went in there, and at school people whispered stories of strange things that had been seen moving through the gloom. Sophie didn't really believe them, but even so she rarely played in the woods, and only that morning her grandpa had warned her again not to go into them. She remembered that now.

We're not really going into the woods, she told herself as she ran to the first oak tree. The key was nestling in its roots. Sophie grabbed it, but as she straightened up, something pale and human-sized seemed to move in the trees. Startled, she stopped and stared. What was that? But the shadows were dark and still again.

Pants! She'd wasted time! Turning round, Sophie climbed back over the fence and raced to the shed, clutching the key. "Home!" she

gasped triumphantly as she hit the shed door with her hand. Sam clicked the stop button.

"So how long did it take me to rescue the magic key?" Sophie demanded.

"One minute, seven point zero four seconds!"

Not bad, Sophie thought. If she hadn't hesitated by the tree then she'd have been even faster. She glanced back at the woods. She'd been *sure* she'd seen something move there. But no, she couldn't have.

"My turn!" Sam chucked her the stopwatch and started to climb nimbly on to the shed roof. Meanwhile, Sophie jogged back to replace the key by the oak tree. As she climbed over the fence, the woods felt strangely still – there wasn't even a single bird singing. Goosebumps prickled over her bare arms.

You're being silly, she told herself firmly. *There's nothing here.*

Placing the key down in the roots of the tree, she headed back to the shed. Sam was waiting on the roof, his blue eyes determined. She lifted the stopwatch. "OK, on your marks... get set... GO!"

"Geronimo!" Sam yelled as he slid down the drainpipe. He was useless at anything that involved a bat or a ball, but he was a fast runner as well as a good climber. He sprinted across the lawn, jumping over the flowerbed. However, he was more cautious then Sophie when it came to finishing the monkey bars. He didn't jump at the end, but climbed down the ladder.

He's slower than me! Sophie thought triumphantly. *I'm going to win!*

Sam reached the oak tree. He rummaged about in the roots. Then he rummaged some more. Finally, he stood up and turned to her. "Where is it?" he shouted indignantly.

Sophie frowned. "What do you mean?"

"It isn't here. Where did you put it?"

Sophie put her hands on her hips. "It *is* there. I put it in the roots."

"Well, I can't see it."

Sophie ran towards him, scrambling over the fence. "I left it just there." She pointed, but to her surprise the space between the tree roots was empty. She stared. Was Sam playing a trick on her? Sophie checked his face. "You really haven't got it?"

"I swear I haven't."

They both began to hunt around, but there

was no sign of the key anywhere. Sophie bit her lip, her eyes wide. "It's gone!"

Sam's face paled. "What's your grandpa going to say?"

Sophie felt sick. Grandpa Bob was not the kindly type of smiley grandpa lots of her friends had – he was grumpy with sharp blue eyes and a grey, grizzled beard. He usually ignored Sophie unless he was telling her off. He much preferred Anthony, Sophie's twin brother. Sophie gulped. She had no idea what Grandpa was going to say – but she had a feeling it wasn't going to be good!

"It can't have just gone," she said desperately. "Let's look again!"

Getting down on their hands and knees, Sophie and Sam began to search.

Deep in the heart of Shadow Woods, Ug the Goblin hurried through the trees. His head was toadstool-shaped and brown rags covered his knobbly body. His snowy-white skin was flaking and tinged black at the edges.

He chortled, hardly believing his luck. He'd done it! He'd got the key! After all these years of watching and waiting! And he hadn't even had to go near the house. Those two stupid children had practically given the key to him – leaving it sitting right where he could take it.

"Dimwits, numskulls, worm brains the lot of them!" he crowed. "But not me. I knew it was the right time to try to steal it. Ug's not King of the Ink Cap Goblins for nothing. Ug's the cleverest and craftiest goblin in the world!" He puffed his chest out. "Ug got the key to the gate. Oh, yes, he did!" His coal-black eyes shone gleefully. Now the shadow creatures' fun could really begin!

2

Anthony the
Annoying

Sophie stared out of her bedroom
window. It was getting late and
beyond the garden fence the
woods were very dark. She hadn't
told Grandpa yet about the key
being lost. He had been out all day
with Anthony, and she was still
hoping the key would turn

up before he discovered it had gone.

Maybe I'll find it tomorrow, she thought hopefully.

Tomorrow. Sophie felt a rush of excitement. Tomorrow was her tenth birthday. Being ten sounded so much older than being nine. What presents would she get? She'd love a new skateboard! And a football, and some games for her DS...

Her bedroom door opened and Anthony strolled in. He looked quite similar to Sophie, with thick, blonde hair and a slim, athletic build, but his eyes weren't green and friendly like hers. They were pale blue and smug.

Sophie frowned. "Hey! Don't just come in without knocking!" She went to the door and pointed to the notice she had stuck there.

"*Private. Keep out. Or you'll be sorry!*" she read.

"Ooh, I'm *so* scared." Anthony rolled his eyes mockingly. He started examining the things on her desk. "I thought you might want to know about my day with Grandpa," he said, flicking through the pages of a tae kwon do book.

"Well, I don't," answered Sophie.

"Really? 'Cos we had a brilliant time," gloated Anthony.

Sophie and Anthony were being looked after by their grandfather for a couple of months. Their parents were archaeologists and often had to go away to work. When that happened, Grandpa moved in. He often took Anthony out to do 'boy-stuff', leaving Sophie at home with the housekeeper, Mrs

Benton. Most of the time, Sophie didn't mind. She loved Mrs Benton and she had much more fun playing with Sam than she would have had being with Anthony and Grandpa.

"You'd have loved it," Anthony went on. "We went climbing on the rocks in the Outwoods and went on the rope swing there. Then after that we had burgers and ice-cream sodas for lunch."

It did sound fun, but there was no way Sophie was going to admit it. "Big deal," she said airily.

But her brother wasn't finished yet. "Before we came home we went to this big outdoor shop. Grandpa bought me a backpack and penknife, a torch and some rope—"

"What?" Sophie burst out, unable to stop

herself. She loved stuff like that – and Anthony knew it. "Did Grandpa get me anything too?"

"No." Anthony laughed. "But I guess that's 'cos you're just a girl."

Sophie clenched her fists angrily.

Anthony grinned. "I reckon Grandpa's planning on taking me camping. You'll get to stay here and have a *lovely* time doing lots of girly things with Mrs Benton," he sniggered. "You could play tea parties together or bath some ickle-wickle baby dolls…"

Sophie gave an enraged yell and leapt at him.

Anthony scrambled over the bed, grabbing a football card from her bedside table as he did so. "Hey, thanks, I need this one!"

"Give it back!"

But Anthony just darted round the bed, past her and through the door.

Sophie glared after him. She wanted to go to his bedroom and snatch the card back, but she'd be bound to be the one who got into trouble. Anthony was *very* good at making it seem as if she started any row between them.

There was the sound of footsteps on the stairs, and then Mrs Benton came in with a tray. On it was a glass of apple juice and a peanut butter sandwich. "I thought you might like a bedtime snack, Sophie-duckie. You didn't eat much at teatime. You're not missing your parents, are you?" the housekeeper asked anxiously.

"Thanks, Mrs B. I'm OK," Sophie replied. The reason she hadn't eaten much was she

had been worrying over Grandpa finding out about his missing key. She wished she could tell Mrs Benton about it, but she knew Mrs B would make her tell Grandpa. Sophie felt sick at the thought.

"Maybe it's just excitement about your birthday then." Mrs Benton smiled fondly at her. She had round, pink cheeks, and had been cooking and cleaning for the Smith family since the twins were babies. "I can't believe you'll be ten tomorrow, Sophie. You won't be too big for a cuddle, will you?" She opened her arms.

Sophie grinned and hugged her. "I'll never be too big for that, Mrs B."

When the housekeeper had gone, Sophie shut her door and got into bed with the sandwich and a book. When she finally got sleepy, she brushed her teeth, turned off her light and snuggled down under the covers.

For a moment, the missing key popped into her head. She forced the thought away and concentrated instead on her birthday.

I hope I do *get a new skateboard,* she thought. Her parents knew it was the only thing she really wanted. Shutting her eyes and imagining herself doing loads of awesome skating tricks, she fell fast asleep.

Happy Birthday Sophie!
We hope you like your
present.
        Lots of love,
        Mum and Dad x x
PS. We went for a camel ride
yesterday; it was exciting
but they don't smell very nice!

Sophie Smith
Keeper's Cottage
Wood Lane
Upper Gately
Warwickshire

LOCATION: THE SANDS OF EGYPT

When Sophie woke in the morning, she felt cold and shivery. As she got out of bed, a wave of dizziness swept over her. "Oh, no," she groaned. She didn't want to be ill on her birthday!

Putting on a pair of jeans and a t-shirt, she went downstairs. When she reached the kitchen, she saw Anthony unwrapping a present. Grandpa was sitting beside him watching, and Mrs Benton was bustling around cooking breakfast.

"Happy birthday, poppet!" Mrs Benton exclaimed, sweeping over.

"Happy birthday, Sophie," Grandpa greeted her, his blue eyes sharp above his grey moustache and short beard. As usual, he didn't look very much like a grandfather. He was slim and fit and dressed all in black, apart from the grey fishing waistcoat with lots of pockets he usually wore.

Anthony held up a digital watch for Sophie to see. "Look what Grandpa's got me! It's got GPS. That means it can tell you where you are and how to get places. Isn't it cool?"

Sophie looked enviously at it. She hoped she'd get one too, but she was sure she wouldn't.

"And this is for you, Sophie," Grandpa

said, handing her a present wrapped in pink ballerina paper. Sophie's heart sank. From the paper she could tell that Grandpa had given Mrs B some money to buy something for her. It felt like clothes. She sat down with the present, still feeling a bit faint.

Grandpa turned back to Anthony. "So, are you feeling OK this morning, Anthony?"

"Yeah, I feel great," Anthony replied.

Sophie blinked, shaking her head. She seemed to have stars dancing in front of her eyes.

"You're quite sure?" she heard Grandpa question Anthony. "You don't feel shivery, faint or light-headed?"

"No."

At that moment, a wave of real dizziness hit Sophie. "I-I do!" she burst out. And with that she fainted.

The next thing Sophie knew, she was being picked up in Grandpa's arms.

"Oh, dear. The poor duckie," Mrs Benton fussed around them. "She must be coming down with something. Anthony, don't open the rest of your presents until Sophie's back downstairs."

"But that's not fair!" Anthony protested. "Just 'cos Sophie's ill, why can't *I* open *my* presents?"

"It's all right, Mrs B," Grandpa said quickly. "He can open them. I'll just take Sophie upstairs and keep an eye on her."

Despite feeling ill, Sophie was astonished. "It's OK, Grandpa," she mumbled. She knew Grandpa would far rather be with Anthony, watching him open his presents. "No, I'm going to look after you,"

Grandpa's voice was firm.

As he carried her up the stairs, he stared at her intently. It was almost as though he was seeing her properly for the first time. "So, it's you," he muttered.

"What?" She wondered if she'd heard him right.

Grandpa reached her bedroom and placed her on her bed. "Have you got a tingling in your arms and legs?" he asked.

She nodded.

"And you're feeling shivery? Dizzy? Seeing stars?"

Sophie stared. How did Grandpa know all that? "Y-yes," she stammered.

Grandpa frowned and shut the door. "Sophie, I've got something very important to tell you." He sat down beside her. "Do you believe in goblins and boggles and trolls – creatures like that?"

She blinked. "What?"

"Do you believe in goblins, boggles and trolls?" Grandpa's face was deadly serious. "Imps, sprites, gnomes and hobgoblins?"

Sophie shook her head. "Of course not! Things like that don't ex—" She'd been about to say *exist,* but Grandpa cut her off.

"They do exist. They're real."

"*Real?*" She sat up, gaping at him.

"Yes."

"But they–they can't be!" Sophie stammered.

"They are," Grandpa said.

Sophie stared at him, her head still swimming. *Maybe I'm dreaming this,* she thought dazedly. Grandpa was behaving so oddly. Creatures like goblins couldn't be real –

they were just in books and fairy tales. She hadn't believed in them since she was about five!

She frowned in confusion. "You're joking, Grandpa—"

"Do I ever joke, Sophie?" he interrupted.

Sophie slowly shook her head. Grandpa was definitely not the joking type.

"Believe me, child. All those creatures live in a dark, frightening place called the Shadow Realm, which lies within the Shadow Woods. Someone has to protect our world against them. That person is known as the Guardian of the Gateway." Grandpa took a deep breath. "And Sophie…"

"Yes?" she said faintly.

Grandpa's blue eyes bored into hers. "From today, that person is you!"

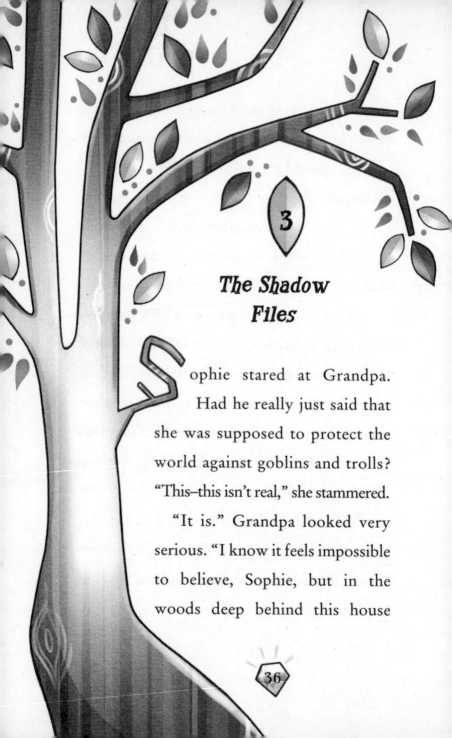

3

The Shadow Files

Sophie stared at Grandpa. Had he really just said that she was supposed to protect the world against goblins and trolls?

"This–this isn't real," she stammered.

"It is." Grandpa looked very serious. "I know it feels impossible to believe, Sophie, but in the woods deep behind this house

there is a magic gateway that leads into the Shadow Realm. The person who is Guardian must stop that gate from ever being opened – because if it *is* ever opened, then the shadow creatures will invade our world."

Sophie swallowed. Grandpa's face was so earnest that she almost found herself believing him. "What would happen then?"

"There would be chaos," Grandpa replied. "Creatures from the Shadow Realm love tricking humans and making them miserable. They steal things and bring dirt, mess and illness. That's why the gate was locked in the first place." He rubbed his beard. "I should start at the beginning. A long time ago, hundreds of years in the past, shadow creatures could pass between our two worlds, but they caused so much mischief that people found a way to lock the gateway. And so they banished all the shadow creatures they could find into the Shadow Realm, and secured the gate from this side."

"So how would the gate ever get opened?" asked Sophie.

"Unfortunately, a few of the creatures escaped and remained in this world, where they lurk in the Shadow Woods. They long to open the gateway again and it's the Guardian's job to stop them – it's *your* job, Sophie."

"But why me?" asked Sophie, still feeling utterly confused.

"The Guardian has always been a member of our family," Grandpa answered. "The role passes down from grandfather to grandchild, with each new Guardian taking over on their

tenth birthday. It has been my job for the last sixty years."

"You, Grandpa!" gasped Sophie.

"Yes." Grandpa rubbed his beard. "So trust me, I know how hard it is to believe all this. When my grandfather told me all about it on my tenth birthday, I thought he must be lying. I don't think I really believed him until I saw my first goblin."

Sophie thought back over the morning. "You didn't think I was going to be the Guardian, did you?" she realised.

"No. I always assumed I would pass the Guardianship on to Anthony." Grandpa looked her up and down as if he still couldn't quite believe it. "A girl... as Guardian! It's never happened before. But you're the one showing all the signs. The dizziness, faintness

39

and seeing stars – those things happened to me and to all the others. You can read about it here." Grandpa pulled a large black notebook out of one of the pockets of his fishing jacket.

Sophie read out the faint gold words on the battered leather cover: "*The Shadow Files.*" She frowned. "What is it?"

Grandpa handed the book to her. "It's a record of the shadow creatures in this world, started by one of the Guardians a long time ago. *The Shadow Files* are yours now. You must record any shadow creature activity, noting the types that you come across."

"What do you mean?" Sophie asked.

Grandpa sighed. "You have so much to learn, child." Sophie found herself wishing that he looked more confident she was going

to learn it! "There are not just goblins, but different types of goblins, like the Marsh Goblins, Tree Goblins, Frost Goblins, Snake Goblins. It is the same with boggles, trolls, sprites, imps and gnomes. So many different types of them and all different to fight." He shuddered. "I can still remember the first time I faced a Wolf Troll."

Sophie felt a flicker of fear. The names of the creatures alone sounded really scary. She remembered the way her skin had crept the day before, when she'd been in the woods and seen something move in the trees. Could that have been a shadow creature?

She cautiously opened *The Shadow Files*. The musty pages whispered lightly through her fingers. The first half of the book was filled with drawings and notes. She stopped

at a hand drawn picture of a squat, warty creature with long ears and a hooked nose. His skin was wrinkled and was coloured-in grey. There was a title saying "Boulder Gnome", and notes in Grandpa's handwriting.

"That was one of the first shadow creatures I ever met," said Grandpa with a slight smile. "You see, these notes will help

42

you if you ever have to fight a Boulder Gnome. Shadow creatures always have some weakness, and once you know what it is, you can use it to defeat them. So you must keep *The Shadow Files* up to date." He flicked through to where there were just blank pages. "Write down everything that happens to you, everything you find out, details of every fight you have."

Sophie bit her lip, still struggling to come to terms with it all. "So... how do I fight them?" she asked cautiously.

"Any way you can." Grandpa looked grim. "It helps that when you're near any type of shadow creature you'll find that your strength and speed increase. You'll be able to kick harder and run faster than you can in normal life."

Sophie felt a sudden thrill of excitement.

Increased speed and strength? That sounded good! "Oh, wow!" she breathed as it all began to seem more real. Her thoughts whirled. Downstairs, she could hear the muffled sounds of Anthony playing with his birthday presents and Mrs B talking to him. What would they say if they knew about all this? What would her parents say?

A thought jumped into her head. "I can't wait to tell Sam!"

"You can't tell him." Grandpa spoke quickly. "No one must know."

"But Sam's my best friend!"

Grandpa shook his head. "I'm afraid ordinary people can't cope with seeing shadow creatures. Children have awful nightmares, and grown-ups try to reason away the evidence of their own eyes.

Sometimes it even sends them mad."

"Sam would be cool with it though," Sophie protested. If she was fighting creatures like goblins and imps, she wanted Sam by her side!

"No, Sophie." Grandpa's voice was absolutely firm. "He must never know."

Sophie's excitement faded slightly. She couldn't imagine having such a big secret and not telling Sam.

"Now, wait here," Grandpa instructed her. "I have something else to show you. Something very important that you must now guard with your very life. It's in my room."

Sophie suddenly felt very cold. As Grandpa swung round and hurried to his room, she was filled with a dreadful sinking feeling. Oh, no, surely it couldn't be...

She heard Grandpa yell. There was the sound of running feet and her bedroom door flew open. Grandpa stood there, his face pale, his eyes shocked. "The key to the gateway!" he exclaimed hoarsely. "It's gone!"

4

The Key to the Gateway

Grandpa held up an empty box. "The key was in here."

Icy fingers ran down Sophie's spine. The box had contained the iron key she and Sam had been playing with. "Oh…" she said slowly.

"Do you know something about

this?" Grandpa strode over to her bed. "Sophie! What happened to it?"

She shrank down under her duvet. "You could say I-I lost it."

Grandpa spoke every word distinctly. "You... *lost*... it?"

Sophie gulped. "Um... yes." She quickly explained to Grandpa what had happened the day before. "One minute it was there by the tree, the next it was gone!" she finished.

"You're telling me you decided to take the key and use it in a *game*?" Grandpa was looking at her as if she had suddenly sprouted three heads. "You put it in Shadow Woods? Where all the shadow creatures live?"

"But I didn't know about that then!" Sophie protested. "And I didn't know it was precious. I—"

"SOPHIE!" Grandpa bellowed. "You've lost the key!"

There was a silence broken only by the sound of Mrs Benton calling up the stairs. "Is everything all right up there?"

Glaring at Sophie, Grandpa strode swiftly to the door. "Yes, everything's fine, Mrs Benton. Sophie and I are just playing a game. She's feeling a lot better now and will be down soon." He turned, shutting the door with a snap.

"We don't know for sure that a shadow creature's taken it, Grandpa," Sophie said.

"What else might it be? A mischievous rabbit?" Grandpa ran his hands through his grey hair. "Of course it was one of the shadow creatures!"

Sophie felt awful. "Does this mean they'll

open the gateway?" Alarm spiralled inside her and she jumped out of bed. "What if they've done it already? What if…?"

"It's all right," Grandpa put a hand on her arm, looking slightly calmer. "Don't worry, the gateway won't be open. The key is made from iron found in our world and a shadow gem from the Shadow Realm. It will only unlock the gate if there is a shadow gem in the hole in its handle. The key on its own can never unlock the gateway."

"Well, in that case it's not so bad they have it then, is it?" said Sophie, looking on the bright side.

Grandpa scowled as if he'd like to shake her. "Not so bad? There are six shadow gems hidden in this world and any one of those gems will make the key work if they are

found. Worst of all, the key can be used to find them if the shadow creatures work out how. We *must* get it back before they manage to get their hands on one of the hidden gems." He glanced out of her window. "I never thought we'd be in this position only hours after I passed the Guardianship on! Come on, we have to get to the gateway."

"What? Now?" said Sophie.

Grandpa nodded. "Now. Whichever shadow creatures stole the key are sure to be there, trying to use it."

Mrs Benton was very pleased to see Sophie come downstairs. "Are you feeling better?"

"Yes, loads better, thanks," Sophie said. It was true. She still felt a bit tingly, but the dizziness had faded. She started to put on her trainers.

"Don't you want to open your presents now?" Mrs Benton asked her.

Sophie realised that she had forgotten all about them! She glanced at the pink ballerina box. "Um, not at the moment. Grandpa and I are just going out."

"Where are you going?" Anthony asked, coming to the kitchen doorway.

"Just for a walk," Grandpa told him. "Come on, Sophie."

Leaving Mrs B and Anthony looking very surprised, they hurried out of the house. Sam was just coming up the driveway on his skateboard, a football-shaped present wrapped in bright blue paper under one arm.

"Happy birthday!" he shouted, sweeping up to Sophie and jumping off his board. "Here you go!" He held out the present. "Bet

you can't guess what it is."

She grinned. "Is it a book?"

Sam grinned back. "Nah, it's a DS game!"

"Come on, Sophie," Grandpa said gruffly, striding off down the garden. "There's no time for presents now."

"Where are you going?" Sam asked Sophie.

Sophie didn't know what to say. She spread her hands. "We're… um… going on a nature walk."

"You? Since when have you liked nature walks? Still, it sounds like fun." Sam joined her. "Let's go."

"You can't come!" Sophie blurted out.

He looked astonished. "Why not?"

"You just can't. I'm really sorry, Sam." She glanced to where Grandpa was climbing over the fence and shoved the present back into

Sam's arms. "It's got to be just me and Grandpa." She saw the flash of hurt in his eyes and felt terrible. "Look, I'll... I'll come round and explain later."

Though I don't know how, she thought as she ran after Grandpa. She left Sam staring after her, the present in his arms.

Grandpa strode through the woods. The paths were overgrown with brambles, and the thick leaves of the trees cut out the light overhead. Grandpa produced two torches from his pockets and handed one to Sophie. "We'll have to get you kitted out," he said. "I bought everything for Anthony yesterday."

Sophie heard the sigh in his voice. She was sure he was still wishing that Anthony had been the Guardian, not her. Determination

filled her. She'd prove to him how good she'd be!

Jumping over the ruts of dried mud, she tried to keep up with him. "So, Grandpa, tell me again about all these special powers I'm going to have now I'm the Guardian. What are they like?"

"You'll be able to run faster and you will have far more strength whenever you're near any type of shadow creature," said Grandpa. "Unfortunately, I won't. The powers can only be with one person at a time and they have now passed on to you. I can give advice and help as much as I can, but you're the one who will have to defeat them." He looked grim at the thought.

Sophie had never been this far into the woods, and it wasn't hard to imagine that

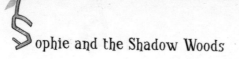

horrible creatures might be lurking in the shadows. As she thought that, her skin started to creep. Maybe they were watching her right now...

Crack! She jumped. It sounded as if someone was following them. "Grandpa! Did you hear that? There was a noise behind us!"

"Do you feel strange?" Grandpa demanded. "Tingly? Full of energy? Like your skin is almost too tight for your body?"

Sophie shook her head.

Grandpa relaxed. "Then it's not a shadow creature. Trust me. You'll know when they are near."

They walked on for another ten minutes until suddenly Sophie felt like she had pins and needles all over her body. She had an intense urge to run and jump and kick and leap. "Grandpa!" she hissed. "I feel strange!"

He nodded. "I thought as much – the gateway is just through those trees in a clearing. And those shadow creatures won't be far away."

He clicked his torch off. Sophie copied him and they crept closer. Grandpa reached the end of the trees and peered through the branches. Putting his finger to his lips, he beckoned Sophie to come up next to him. "I think we've found our thieves."

She parted the tree branches.

"Ink Cap Goblins," Grandpa whispered.

Sophie caught her breath. Four goblins were standing in a small clearing! They were taller than her – but not quite as tall as Grandpa. They had pointy heads and their flaky skin was so white that it seemed to glow in the dim light, apart from at the edges of their body where it looked black and rotting. They had large, fat noses and dark

eyes. One of them seemed to be the leader. He wore a mouldy black cloak, and the other three were all looking at him as if expecting answers.

"Well, *I* don't know why it's not working!" he exclaimed. Sophie's heart flipped. He was holding the key! "It's not like it comes with instructions." He strode up and down angrily.

"We are sure our great king, Ug, will find a way to make the key work," fawned one of the others, with a nose so knobbly it looked like a potato.

"Yes, Great King Ug is the most clever of all goblins!" grovelled another with a particularly flaky face.

"His genius is beyond compare," said the third, who had large bulbous feet.

Ug stopped and preened. "Ug is indeed the

most clever of the goblins. You are right. I *will* think of a way." He turned to a space between two trees and started waving the key about madly.

Sophie stared. She could see the air between the trees shimmering with a golden haze. "Is that the gateway?" she whispered to Grandpa.

"Yes," he hissed. "It's good there are only four of them, and that they're Ink Cap Goblins. Ink Caps are easily injured and quite cowardly."

"Great!" said Sophie. She could hardly wait to try out her new powers. Already she felt so tingly with strength that she could hardly sit still.

Grandpa glowered at her. "Not so fast. You see those inky black bits on their arms? They can squeeze poisonous liquid from them that will blister your skin if it touches you. *Don't* let them get their hands on you – just get that key back!" Grandpa's gaze met hers. "Do you think you can do it?"

"Yes!" Sophie declared hotly. "I'll use my tae kwon do moves!"

For a moment, a smile flickered across Grandpa's face. "Good girl. Now get going!"

5

Captured

As Grandpa and Sophie strode out into the clearing, the goblins all shouted in alarm.

"We want the key back," Grandpa declared.

"It's the Guardian!" exclaimed King Ug, his white skin turning even paler. "With a... with a..." He frowned and blinked, the panic leaving him. "With a *girl*!"

Sophie swallowed. Now that she was actually in the clearing, the four goblins seemed very large. But there was no way she was going to seem frightened. "I'm the Guardian now," she said, trying to sound braver than she felt.

The goblins gaped at her. One by one, they turned and stared at Grandpa, who nodded. "It's true," he said heavily. Sophie winced, wishing that he sounded more pleased about it!

Flaky Face's mouth dropped open. "The new Guardian's a girl?"

"*She* can't be the new Guardian," said Potato Nose.

Big Feet didn't say anything at all. He just

stared at Sophie, looking stunned.

"A girl Guardian!" A grin spread across Ug's face. "This is wonderful, excellent. Oh, yes, yes, yes!" He rubbed his hands together gleefully. "Ug's day gets better and better!"

Sophie felt a flash of anger. She pulled her shoulders back and gave Ug a challenging look. "OK, I'm a girl. So what?"

Ug smirked round at the other goblins. "Aww, the little girl's talking to us. We'd better not upset her. She might hit us with her dolly!"

The others roared with laughter.

"Or tie us up with her hair ribbons," sniggered Ug. "Or make us have a tea party!"

The goblins whooped.

Sophie felt as if power was filling every

cell in her body. She longed to run and spin
and kick.

Grandpa seemed to read her mind.
"Steady, Sophie," he warned in a low voice.
"You don't know the full extent of your
powers yet. It'll take you a little while to
get used to them."

Ug turned back to Sophie, his black eyes
glittering. "Skip home now and make us
some cakes, little girl, and maybe we'll be
very nice and not hurt you."

"I'm not going home without the key,"
said Sophie.

The goblin leader waved it tauntingly at
her. "If you want it, come and get it!"

"Thanks." Sophie smiled. "I will."

She moved so that one foot was in front of
the other, and brought her arms up into the

ready position, just as she did every week in her tae kwon do class.

"Ooh, we're doing ballet!" crowed Ug, copying her. The others fell about laughing.

Sophie darted forward at lightning speed and kicked out. Ug ducked back just in time. For a split second, Sophie saw the surprise on his face, and then she was spinning round ready for her next move. She had never felt so strong! She shot her right leg up into a high kick. This time, the outer part of her foot connected firmly with Ug's squishy chest. "Waaaaa!" the King yelled, flying backwards through the air.

Sophie was buzzing. She didn't care that there were so many goblins. She could fight them all! She ran straight at them, planning to attack with a flying side kick. It was a very difficult move, but right then, she felt like she could do anything! She sprang into the air, turning her body to the side.

"Be careful, Sophie!" Grandpa shouted.

But Grandpa's warning came too late. With her new power surging through her, Sophie couldn't control her jump. She flew through the air – straight over the goblins' heads!

CRASH! She hit a tree on the other side of the goblins, her head colliding with a branch before she fell into a heap on the ground.

Grandpa reached her in seconds and crouched down. "Sophie! Are you all right?"

Sophie sat up groggily, gasping for air. She could tell she wasn't badly hurt, just winded from the fall and dazed from banging her

head. She'd been winded once before in class and she knew it would take a few minutes before she could breathe normally again.

"Deep breaths, child," Grandpa told her, his hand firm on her shoulder.

Ug was dusting himself down, trying to recover his composure. "Huh!" he muttered. "Well, I guess you're not so bad – for a girl. But you'll never get the key. Tie them up!" he ordered.

The other goblins broke off long ropes of twisting ivy from the trees and closed in on Grandpa. He yelled and struggled, but there were three of them and only one of him. Their white fingers grasped his arms, swiftly tying his hands behind him and his legs together.

Sophie struggled to her feet. "No!" she

panted. What if they used their poison? Her head spun. She just needed a few minutes to get herself together. But she didn't have a few minutes. The three goblins pushed her back down to the ground. As Sophie fell, a sudden flash of colour in a nearby tree caught her eye. What was that?

The next second, a football wrapped in bright blue paper was shooting through the clearing straight towards Ug's head! Seeing it fall short of its target, Sophie instantly knew who had thrown it. Only one person could be such a bad shot...

"Sam!" she gasped.

"GERONIMO!" Sam yelled, sliding down the tree trunk.

The goblins swung round as Sam dropped lightly to his feet on the ground.

"Don't worry, Sophie!" he shouted. "I'll save you and your grandpa from those… things!" His face was pale, but his eyes were determined as he ran towards them, jumping over a tree stump in his way.

"Don't just stand there, you numskulls!" shrieked Ug. "Get him!" All four Ink Cap Goblins ran towards Sam, their fleshy bodies wobbling.

Sophie had no idea how Sam had come to be there, but right now all that mattered was fighting the goblins. Sam's sudden appearance had given her the time she needed. Her breath was slowly coming back and her head was clearing. She got to her feet.

Just as the goblins reached him, Sam scooted up a tree trunk. Flinging himself on to one of the lower branches, he swung away as if he was going along the monkey bars in Sophie's garden. The goblins shook their fists and yelled. Their attention was so fixed on him that they'd forgotten Sophie for the moment.

"*Geronimo!*" she muttered, and the next second she was running straight towards them like an arrow fired from a bow. A few metres away from the goblins she leapt into the air again, this time controlling her speed and height. Turning sideways, she kicked out with her right foot, knocking Ug to the ground.

As he sprawled over, she landed in perfect balance. "Take that!" she yelled.

The other goblins drew back in alarm.

Rushing forward, Sophie spun round again, kicking out high with her right foot

and knocking Flaky Face over with a satisfying *splat*. "And that!" she shouted.

The other two goblins had seen enough. They ran off into the trees, howling. Seconds

73

later, Ug and Flaky Face had scrambled to their feet and followed them.

"You did it!" yelled Sam, dropping down from the branches. "You scared those things off!"

Sophie ran to the edge of the clearing where the goblins were running away through the trees. "Ha!" she yelled, triumph beating through her. "So I'm *just* a girl, am I? Well, you'll never find any of those hidden gems that make the key open the gateway. Never!"

Ug stopped and stared at her just as Grandpa shouted, "NO!"

"Gems!" The King's eyes lit up with understanding. "That explains why the gateway wouldn't open! We need to find a shadow gem and when we have one, the key

will work…" He gave a delighted laugh and rubbed his hands. "Ug'll be seeing you around, little girl." And with that, he disappeared into the shadows after the others.

Sophie clapped her hands to her mouth. How could she have told them about the gems?

"SOPHIE!" Grandpa roared.

She turned slowly.

Sam had untied Grandpa, who now came marching across the clearing. "You harebrained, muddle-headed child! Do you know what you've done? Those goblins will stop at nothing to find one of the six hidden gems now!"

"I—I'm sorry!" Sophie gasped.

Grandpa buried his head in his hands. "I *knew* the Guardian should have been

Anthony. First you lose the key, and now this. And it's only day one!"

"I'll sort it, Grandpa," Sophie said desperately. "I'll get the key back from them and I won't let them find the gem. I *will* be a good Guardian – I will!"

Grandpa groaned despairingly.

Behind them, Sam cleared his throat. "Um… would someone please tell me what's going on?"

6

A Secret
Mission

ver Grandpa's protestations,
Sophie quickly told Sam everything
about the goblins, the gateway,
the key and the six hidden gems.

Sam's eyes widened to the
size of soup plates. "Oh, wow!
Well, if you're this Guardian
person, I'm going to help. We'll be

like Batman and Robin!"

"No, no, no!" Grandpa looked about as keen on that idea as having a goblin come round for supper. "The Guardian always works alone, Sophie," he said. "The only person that helps him – I mean *her* – is the old Guardian."

Sophie pursed her lips. "Well, not any longer. Sam's in, Grandpa, or I'm not going to be Guardian."

Their eyes clashed. Sophie still had the lingering feelings of power from when the goblins had been there and she was determined not to back down.

Grandpa's frown deepened. "Oh, very well," he snapped. "But on your own heads be it!"

78

"What were you thinking of, going on a nature ramble when the poor child's not well?" Mrs Benton hurried out of the house as she saw them coming back through the garden.

"I'm OK now, Mrs B," called Sophie. The faint and dizzy feelings had long gone.

"Look at the state of you all!" the housekeeper exclaimed, catching sight of a tear in Sophie's jeans and a rip in Sam's jumper. "What *have* you been doing?"

"Just playing," said Grandpa swiftly. "Children will be children."

"You know, I'm ever so hungry, Mrs B," said Sam. "Do you have any biscuits?"

His distraction worked perfectly. "Of course I do, Sam," Mrs B smiled. "Fresh out of the oven. Come inside."

She led the way into the kitchen. Grandpa caught Sophie's arm. "Sophie, can I have *The Shadow Files?*" he hissed. "I must check something."

She nodded and quickly handed it over.

"Good girl. I will see you in a few minutes."

Wondering what he wanted *The Shadow Files* for, Sophie followed Mrs B and Sam. Anthony was at the table playing on his DS. He groaned when he saw Sam. "Oh, no, not him. Does he have to be here on my birthday?"

Sam and Anthony didn't get on at all. In fact, Anthony and his gang of cool friends often picked on Sam at school.

"Now, Anthony, don't be unfriendly," Mrs Benton said.

As she turned away to get the biscuits, Anthony flicked an old, dried-up pea across

the table at Sam. Sam scowled and ignored him.

Sophie saw her presents and went over.

"I wouldn't bother," Anthony smirked. "Most of them are rubbish!"

Sophie realised that her brother had pulled up a flap of wrapping paper on each of her gifts to see what was inside. "You looked at them!" she said indignantly.

"Sorry." He didn't sound anything of the sort.

Sophie glared at him and started unwrapping her presents as Mrs B brought the biscuits and juice over to the table. The best thing by far was the new skateboard her mum and dad had given her. She grinned as she examined it.

Just then, Grandpa appeared in the doorway. His clothes were tidy once more and his grey hair smoothed down.

"Hey, Grandpa, can you show me how to work my watch now?" Anthony asked.

But Grandpa shook his head. "Sorry, Anthony, but I have to go out to the shops. I need to get something for Sophie."

"For Sophie!" Anthony exclaimed. "Why?"

Grandpa didn't answer. "Can I have a quick word with you, Sophie?"

She nodded. As Grandpa led her out of the

82

kitchen, Sophie saw Anthony's stunned face and Sam's interested one. "I'll be right back, Sam," she said over her shoulder as Grandpa shut the door firmly behind them.

Grandpa lowered his voice. "I need to tell you more about the six gems."

Sophie nodded eagerly.

"When the first Guardian was forging the key," Grandpa told her, "he brought six different-coloured gems out of the Shadow Realm into this world, unsure which of the six would be the best to use in the key. Then, when the key was finished, he discovered that any of the six gems would work if placed in the hole in the handle. Once he knew this, he used magic to hide them all."

"But why?" said Sophie.

Grandpa rolled his eyes. "In order to

protect against exactly the type of situation that has happened today, of course, child! The goblins may have managed to steal the key, but they can't open the gateway because they don't have a gem to fit into the handle – and because the gate is shut they can't get into the Shadow Realm to get one. We must protect the six hidden gems at all costs."

"Where are they?" Sophie asked.

"I don't know. I've never needed to find them. This is the first time the key has fallen into the wrong hands." He gave her a hard look, and Sophie gulped. She was never going to hear the end of that! "In any event, I was told by my grandfather that there are clues as to their whereabouts scattered on pages throughout *The Shadow Files*," Grandpa went on. "Like this one."

He pushed *The Shadow Files* into her hand,

open at the page on the Boulder Gnomes. He pointed at four lines of writing at the bottom of the page. Sophie read them to herself:

In a rose-covered cottage
The green gem will be found
Hidden in a cellar
Deep under the ground.

"Rose-covered cottage?" Sophie breathed. "Could that be Mrs B's cottage? It has roses all over it. And it's got a cellar!"

Grandpa nodded. "I think it does sound as if the green gem may be there. While I'm out, I want you to watch Mrs B's cottage in case any Ink Cap Goblins come snooping around. We can think about a safer hiding place when I get back."

Sophie nodded.

"Guard the gem with your life," Grandpa told her.

85

Sophie felt solemn with the seriousness of it all. "I will," she promised.

"Good." Grandpa fixed her with a penetrating stare. "And try not to make any mistakes this time, Sophie. You've made enough already today." He left, shutting the front door with a bang.

Sophie wondered what to do with *The Shadow Files*. It was too big to go in her pocket, but she didn't want to leave it lying around. Fetching a small denim backpack she slipped the book inside and put it on her back.

"What's up with Grandpa this morning?" Anthony looked disgruntled as Sophie went back into the kitchen. "Taking you out for a walk, telling you private things in the hall. What's going on?"

"Nothing." Sophie picked up her skateboard and glanced at Sam. "Should we go outside?"

"Sure," Sam said, jumping to his feet. They went out through the front door. "What did your grandpa want to talk to you about?" he hissed the moment it had shut behind them.

"He told me about the six gems! They're different colours and hidden all over the place, and there are riddles in *The Shadow Files* that tell us where they are. Grandpa found one and we worked it out. It's—" Sophie broke off as Anthony came out too. She and Sam waited as he got his bike.

"What are you two looking at?" he asked suspiciously.

"Nothing," said Sophie quickly, eager for him to go. "Have a nice time, wherever

87

you're going. Bye!"

Anthony frowned. "You're acting so weird today. Even weirder than normal, and that's saying something." Giving her a thoughtful look, he cycled off down the driveway.

Sophie spun back towards Sam. "Right. This clue Grandpa found. It's a green gem, and we think it's in the cellar of Mrs B's cottage!"

Sam gasped. "That doesn't sound a very safe hiding place!"

"I know. Grandpa said we have to keep it safe until he gets back. We've got to keep an eye out for—" She heard the sound of a bike and looked round. Anthony had come back. He stopped at the bottom of the drive.

"OK, what's going on?"

"Going on?" Sophie echoed innocently.

"Yeah. All that stuff with Grandpa, and now

look at you – whispering together. What's the big secret?"

"No big secret, we're just playing a game," said Sam.

Anthony's eyes narrowed. He didn't look convinced.

"Oh, just go away!" Sophie told him, losing patience.

With a shrug, her twin brother cycled off.

"Phew!" said Sophie, pretending to wipe off her forehead. She was a bit surprised, though, that Anthony had given up so easily. "Come on, we'd better get started watching the cottage," she said to Sam.

Getting on their skateboards they skated down the lane. Sophie's street was a very quiet one, with trees lining one side of it. Her house was the last one where the lane finished, and Sam's was at the other end near the main road. Mrs Benton lived halfway between them.

"I can't believe it's hidden in Mrs B's cellar!" said Sam as they glided along. "Sssh!" said Sophie quickly as the bushes nearby rustled. But it couldn't be a shadow creature or her superstrength would have kicked in. *It must have just been a bird or a squirrel,* she thought in relief. "We'd better keep our voices down," she warned Sam. He nodded.

As they swooped into Mrs Benton's drive, her cottage looked just as it always did, with tubs full of bright flowers outside the door, and a small shed where Mrs B kept her lawnmower.

"I can't see any goblins," Sam whispered.

"And I don't feel all strange and tingly,"

said Sophie, letting out a thankful breath.
"There mustn't be any here."

They hung around for a bit, but it was
quite boring so they decided to play on their
skateboards back on Sophie's driveway,

where there was a small skateboard ramp.

"We can keep coming back here and checking," said Sophie. They skated back and started to practise some jumps called ollies.

"Right, I'm going to do a kick flip now!" said Sophie. But as she pushed her weight down so that she could jump and spin the board beneath her, she suddenly felt a tingling, rushing sensation. Instead of jumping slightly above the board, she flew two metres into the air! Her arms flailed as she came crashing down with a surprised yell.

"Are you OK?" Sam raced over. "What happened? You shot up like a rocket!"

"Shadow creatures!" gasped Sophie, springing to her feet. "There must be shadow creatures around right now!"

7

Danger!

Sam glanced round. "Goblins? Where?"

Horror rushed through Sophie. "Mrs B's cottage!" She sprinted off down the drive.

"Wait for me!" Sam shouted. But even on his skateboard he could barely keep up. Sophie tore down the lane, the feeling of power growing stronger inside her. She couldn't see any goblins yet, but she did spot something propped against Mrs B's gateway – a bike.

"That's Anthony's!" she said as they raced along. "He must be here!"

A horrible thought came to her as she remembered the rustling in the bushes. Anthony had been spying on them! He must have heard them say something was hidden in Mrs B's cellar. Now he'd come here to find out what it was. And there were shadow creatures nearby!

Sophie swung into the driveway. Sure enough, Anthony was there. The shed, where Mrs B kept her spare key, was open – and Anthony's back was to them as he unlocked the front door.

Sophie caught her breath as she saw the four Ink Cap Goblins creeping out from the bushes on either side of the garden. Their beady eyes were fixed on Anthony and the door. Remembering Grandpa's warning, one thought filled Sophie's mind – she couldn't let Anthony see the goblins!

She pounded up the drive just as Anthony swung open the front door. Her twin spun round, looking cross. "What are you doing he—"

The 'here' was drowned out as Sophie launched herself at him in a rugby tackle, sending him crashing to the ground and knocking the key from his hand.

"What are you doing, you idiot? Get off me!" He thrashed around, trying to kick and punch her, but with her superstrength she held him down easily.

There was only one thing for it. Jumping to her feet, she threw him over her back in a fireman's lift.

"Stop it!" Anthony shrieked as she hurtled towards the shed's open door. "Put me down!"

"Sure!" Sophie dumped him inside the shed, pulled the door shut, slammed the bolt across and dusted down her hands.

"Let me out! I'll tell Grandpa! LET ME OUT!" Anthony hammered on the door, but Sophie had other things on her mind. The four goblins were hurrying towards the open front door.

"You stop right there!" shouted Sophie, marching over to them.

"Be careful!" Sam called anxiously from the driveway.

The goblins all swung round. Ug rolled his black eyes. "Oh, not you again." He looked warier than before, but he didn't back away from her. "Shouldn't you be in your bedroom making fairy wings?" The other three goblins sniggered.

Getting between the goblins and the porch of the cottage, Sophie slammed the door shut and folded her arms over her chest. "You're not going in Mrs B's house," she told them.

"Oh, but we are," said Ug. "You see, we were on our way to your house when I noticed something." He held the key out. It was tied on a chain round his neck, and was shining with a green light. "When we got near *this* house, the key started to glow... and the closer we've got to the door, the brighter it has become. Now, why would that be?"

Sophie bit her lip. The key must glow when it was close to the missing gems. Grandpa hadn't warned her about that!

"And why would you be so keen to stop us going inside if there wasn't something very special in there – something you didn't want us to find?" The King's lumpy face looked crafty. "Ug's clever, he is. Too clever for you! There's a shadow gem in that house and Ug's going to get it."

"Just try it," said Sophie, not moving.

"She can't count!" chortled Ug to his cronies. "Look, little girl, there's…" he turned to the other goblins and counted them, "one, two, three, *four* of us. How exactly are you going to stop us when there's… let me see, just *one* of you?"

"I'm here too!" called Sam, skating closer.

"Sophie's not on her own. If you want to get in there you'll have to get past me as well!"

Ug rubbed his hands. "You know, I was really hoping you'd say that!" He glanced at Flaky Face and nodded.

Before Sophie could do anything, the ugly goblin had lunged at Sam, lifting him off his board and throwing him through the air. Sam yelled in surprise as he landed at the bottom of the tree that held up Mrs Benton's washing line.

"Sam!" Sophie gasped as the goblins all whooped and laughed.

"I'm OK," Sam called, starting to scramble to his feet.

Sophie felt a wave of hot anger. "Right, that's it!" she said furiously. "You're asking for trouble!"

"Oooh, I'm so scared!" mocked Ug. "GET HER, YOU THREE!" he yelled.

The three other goblins charged forward, Flaky Face in the lead, Big Feet and Potato Nose just behind.

Wait, wait... Sophie told herself, remembering all her tae kwon do lessons.

She didn't move until Flaky Face was so close she could smell the scent of rotting compost coming from him. *Now!* she thought. She kicked out with her left foot, following immediately through with her right in a double kick. *Thwack! Thunk!* Her feet thudded into Flaky Face's chest with all her superstrength, sending him shooting backwards.

"ARGH!" he yelled as he collided with the water butt. It toppled over, spilling slimy

green water all over him.

"Way to go, Sophie!" Sam shouted, punching the air.

The other two goblins had paused, but now they roared and came at her. Sophie spun round, kicking out with her back foot and catching Potato Nose on the shoulder. He sprawled over just as she sent Big Feet flying with a second double kick. He landed among the flowerpots with a crash and sat up groaning, a pink petunia sitting on his head.

Sam laughed in delight. "Loooosers!"

Sophie turned to Ug, grinning broadly. "You were right, you know. It wasn't a fair fight, was it? But now it's just you and me." She twirled the end of her long, blonde ponytail and looked at him. "Unless of course you think you'd rather leave."

As Ug backed away, she saw his eyes flicker over her shoulder. "Ah well, maybe we should be sensible about this—"

"Sophie! Potato Nose is up!" Sam yelled.

Sophie heard the sound of feet behind her and jumped to one side. Potato Nose's arms closed on empty air. But the sudden move had unbalanced Sophie, and Potato Nose swung round, butting her in the stomach with his head. The air *whooshed*

102

past her as she flew backwards, landing with a thud on the ground near the tree with the washing line. Potato Nose started running towards her.

"Get on the other side of the washing line!" Sam's voice yelled. He sounded as if he was somewhere above her.

Sophie quickly did as he said, and as Potato Nose reached the tree, the line came tumbling down. The next minute the goblin was stumbling about, caught up in Mrs B's dresses and tights. "Gaaah!" he

shouted, batting away a long, frilly nightie.

"*Yes!*" exclaimed Sophie.

"Got him!" Sam hollered at the same time.

Looking around, Sophie saw Flaky Face staggering to his feet, drenched with slimy water. Nearby, Big Feet was groaning as he climbed out of the broken flowerpots. Potato Nose still had a pair of tights dangling from his shoulder and a pair of Mrs B's large pants caught on one of his ears!

"Right, we can do this the easy way or the hard way," Sophie told the three goblins firmly. "Either you go now or Sam and I fight you some more. Which is it to be?"

They all shuffled backwards.

"I'll give you five seconds to decide," Sophie said. "One. Two... Oops, sorry," she said. "I forgot that you told me I can't count,

can I? FIVE!" she yelled, and started running towards them.

Shouting in fear, the three goblins stampeded down the drive. Sophie grinned. "We did it!" she said as Sam joined her on his skateboard. "We got rid of them." They high-fived.

"Wait a minute," said Sam suddenly. "Where's Ug?"

Sophie had assumed that the goblin king had run away as well, while she was fighting the others. She grinned as she glanced around. "Oh, he's probably still run…" She slowly trailed off, her eyes widening in horror.

Behind them, the front door stood wide open.

8

Saving the Day

Sophie and Sam ran into Mrs B's cottage. "This way!" cried Sophie, heading for the kitchen. As they entered the room, she saw that the door to the cellar stairs stood open. A ghostly green light was shining upwards. Ug was in there!

They thudded down the wooden staircase. Mrs B's cellar had stone walls and was filled with odds and ends. Ug was stalking around the room, waving the glowing key about as he searched for the gem.

"Stop right there!" bellowed Sophie.

Ug spun round. "You again!" he snapped. "You really are a very tiresome child. Well, you're not going to stop me now!"

"Want to bet?" Sophie demanded. But even as she was speaking, Ug was running the key along the wall. As the key touched a small, loose-looking stone, the green light suddenly grew so strong that Sophie gasped, shading her eyes.

"Got it!" crowed Ug. He prised the stone out of the wall with his long, thin fingers... and to Sophie's dismay, there was a green gem!

"NO!" she shouted. Just as Ug reached for the gem, she launched herself through the air at him, spinning round in a high kick. *Thwack!* The goblin went skidding across the floor. The gem rolled out of his hand.

"Sam, grab it!" cried Sophie. Sam started forward – but before he could reach the gem, Ug had snatched it up again.

"Give me that gem back," said Sophie in a low voice. She took a step towards him.

"Stay away, little girl – or else!" sneered Ug. Snatching up an empty bucket, he started carefully squeezing the edges of his arms. Black gunge dripped into the plastic bucket.

"Ew, *disgusting*," breathed Sam.

Sophie stopped in her tracks, watching in horrified fascination. Then suddenly she remembered what Grandpa had told her.

That inky goo could burn their skin!

Ug held up the bucket, his black eyes gleaming. "I've had it up to my ears with you two. No one is going to stop Ug from leaving with this gem. No one!" And holding the bucket high, the goblin king took aim... and fired.

Sophie stood frozen as the dark, poisonous contents of the bucket came hurtling towards her. She could hear the black goo bubbling, like boiling water. Her superstrength couldn't help her against this. She was about to be burned!

"No!" Sam yelled.

Grabbing an empty paint can, he leapt into the air with it outstretched. The gunge made a splattering noise as it landed inside the can. Taking aim, Sam chucked it straight back the goblin. "Take that!" he shouted.

"ARGGHH!" howled Ug as the black goo splashed on to his pale skin. He dropped the gem as he shrieked and danced about.

It rolled across the room, and Sophie quickly scooped it up. It was small and many-faceted, like a glittering marble.

"Sam, that was brilliant," she gasped, spinning towards him. "You actually caught the goo!"

He looked stunned. "I've never caught anything in my life!"

Meanwhile, Ug was still yelping in dismay. The black splodges were fizzling as they spread all over his body, like ink on damp tissue paper. "Look what you've done to me, you stupid children!" he bellowed. He shook his fist at them. "You'll be sorry for this! You'll be sorry!" He ran away up the stairs.

Sophie shoved the gem into her jeans pocket. "Come on, after him!"

She and Sam raced back up the stairs and through the house. As they burst outside, she saw Ug pelting down the driveway. Just then, Grandpa turned into the drive with a carrier bag in his hands. Ug dodged past him, disappearing into the woods on the other side of the lane.

"Grandpa!" cried Sophie, running to meet him.

"What's been happening?" He strode towards them in alarm. "That was Ug!"

"Yes, we've been fighting him and the others," she burst out. "They were trying to get the green gem!"

"Did you stop them?" Grandpa asked anxiously. Sophie dug into her jeans pocket and held the gem up. It winked in the sunlight. Her grandfather

heaved out a sigh. "Well done!"

"LET ME OUT!" came a voice from behind them.

Grandpa swung round. "What's that noise? Is there a goblin locked in the shed?"

She and Sam looked at each other. "Um… no. That's Anthony," said Sophie. "It's a long story." As they told Grandpa what had been happening, a faint smile crossed his gruff face.

"You both did well," he said. "Ink Caps are some of the easier goblins to fight, but it was brave of you to tackle all four of them." His expression became more serious again. "But I hope you've learned some valuable lessons, because next time you might not be so lucky. Never take your eyes off a shadow creature, and *never* go into battle without weapons."

"We *did* have weapons – Mrs B's washing and an old paint can," said Sophie. "Plus, Sam actually caught something for the first time in his life!" she teased, nudging her friend. He grinned, obviously pleased with himself.

Grandpa didn't look amused. "This is no laughing matter. You must remember the three vital words when it comes to fighting goblins: Prepare, prepare, prepare…"

Sophie frowned. "Um, that's just one word, Grandpa."

He shook his head in exasperation and strode away to unbolt the shed door. Anthony came stalking out, his hair dusty and full of cobwebs. "What did you do that for, you—"

He broke off as he saw who it was. "Grandpa! Sophie locked me in the shed! I

was in there for ages." He shot Sophie a look as if to say, *Now you're in* big *trouble...*

Grandpa patted Anthony's shoulder. "Well, well, I'm sure you'll be fine." He turned round and wagged his finger. "Sophie, you mustn't lock your brother in sheds. Do you understand?"

Sophie bit back a grin. "Yes, Grandpa. Sorry." She sounded about as sorry as Anthony had when he'd apologised for sneaking a look into her birthday presents. Anthony glared at her.

"We'll say no more about it then," Grandpa declared.

"But Grandpa, you've got to punish them! They were going to get into Mrs B's house to look for something hidden in the cellar. I heard them say it!"

"Something hidden..." Grandpa shook his

head and laughed. "Oh, dearie me, you should know better than to believe your sister's games, Anthony." He looked at Sophie and Sam. "Now, you two, did you go into Mrs B's house looking for something?"

"No," Sophie answered honestly. They had gone into the cellar to stop Ug, not to look for the gem.

"That's because they were too busy playing stupid games out here, locking me in and making loads of noise – and look!" Anthony's voice rose as he pointed to the broken flowerpots and the disturbed washing. "What's Mrs B going to say about *that,* huh, Sophie?"

Sophie's heart sank as she looked around her. Anthony had a point… though she was more worried about the splatters of black goo in the cellar!

"It certainly seems as if you two have some clearing up to do," said Grandpa to her and Sam. "Stay here and try and get everything in order, please. I'm taking Anthony home. If there's… er, anything else that needs doing, I'll help you with it when I get back. Do you understand?"

Sophie nodded in relief. Picking up the key from the ground, Grandpa locked the front door and slipped the key into his pocket. "Mrs B really shouldn't leave this lying around. There's no knowing who might try and get in. Oh, and Sophie…" Grandpa threw the plastic bag in her direction, "this is for you."

"Thanks." Sophie caught it. Giving her a wink, Grandpa steered Anthony away.

"What is it?" Sam asked as soon as Grandpa and Anthony were out of earshot.

Looking inside the plastic bag, Sophie pulled out a GPS watch and a black sleeveless jacket with lots of pockets. "Oh, wow! Cool!" She took off her backpack, put the jacket on and slipped *The Shadow Files* into one of its pockets. Suddenly she felt like a proper Guardian.

"Can I borrow the watch sometime?" Sam asked.

"Of course you can," said Sophie, strapping the watch on. She turned her wrist from side to side, admiring it. "We can share it."

Sam started to pick up the washing. "It was lucky Mrs B wasn't at home today. We'll have to hide this gem somewhere else now. It's not safe to keep it here any longer."

"I don't think anywhere's going to be safe now the goblins know the key glows like that when they're near a gem," said Sophie. She frowned. "I think I should keep it with me."

"But then they'll come after you!"

"I know, but my superpowers will let me know when they're around, and help me to defend myself." She put the gem away in one of the inside pockets of the jacket and looked at him. "It makes sense. We should try and solve the riddles and get all the gems back. Then when we've managed to get the key from the goblins we can maybe hide them in safe places again."

Sam nodded slowly. "We absolutely can't let Ug get his hands on them. I wonder if other shadow creatures will hear about the key, and if we'll have to fight them too?"

Sophie pulled the book out and flicked through its pages. "Look – Fog Trolls, Slime Imps, Swamp Boggles, Bat Goblins…" As she looked at the different pictures of the menacing, ugly creatures, she swallowed. Grandpa had said Ink Caps were some of the easiest to fight. How was she ever going to defeat all these other horrible-looking shadow creatures?

Sam saw her face. "We'll be OK," he said, but his voice shook just slightly.

"Of course we will. I mean, all we've got to do is fight a load of big, mean creatures, stop them finding six magic gems, which they want to use to unlock a gateway into the Shadow Realm that they *really* want to open…" Sophie had to grin at the thought. "What's so hard about that?"

"Nothing – nothing at all."

As Sam grinned back, Sophie felt better. Whatever shadow creatures came along, she knew she and Sam would be waiting for them and would face them side by side. She gazed down the drive towards the woods. "We're ready for you, all you goblins, boggles and trolls!" she declared.

"And you imps, sprites and gnomes too!" Sam joined in bravely. "Any time you want!"

Sophie flicked back her ponytail. "Just bring it on!"

Deep in the trees, Ug glared angrily at the splodges on his skin as he plotted and schemed. He'd had one of the shadow gems

right in his hand! How dare those irritating children get in the way of his plans? Well, he would have his revenge on them... *and* find one of those gems to fit into the key, no matter what it took!

"The new Guardian and her friend haven't seen the last of Ug," he muttered to himself, rubbing his hands together. "Ug will be back. Oh, yes, Ug will be back..."

THE
SHADOW
FILES

- Find its weakness
- Wait for the Guardian powers to kick in...
  and then attack!

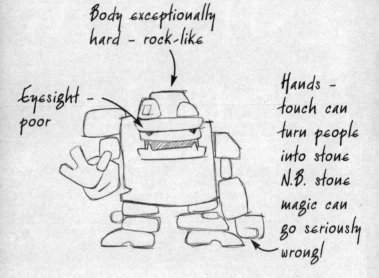

Body exceptionally
hard - rock-like

Eyesight -
poor

Hands -
touch can
turn people
into stone
N.B. stone
magic can
go seriously
wrong!

HOW TO FIGHT A BOULDER GNOME

- Roll down hill and then they will
  shatter at bottom.
- Hit them with a sledgehammer

In a rose-covered cottage
The green gem will be found
Hidden in a cellar
Deep under the ground.

The Key to the Gateway

made of iron

hole in middle where a shadow gem goes

unlocks the magic gateway into the Shadow Realm

N.B. Very precious. DON'T LOSE!!

Famous
Superheroes and
their Partners –

Sophie and Sam
            OF COURSE!
Batman and Robin,

The Incredibles,

Sherlock Holmes

and Watson

Wallace
and
Gromit

INK CAP GOBLIN

DON'T LET THEM SNEAK UP ON YOU!

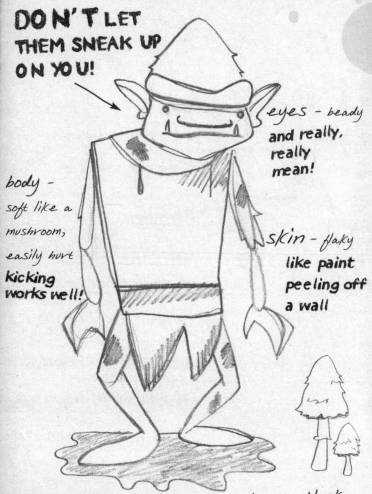

eyes - beady and really, really mean!

body - soft like a mushroom, easily hurt **kicking works well!**

skin - flaky like paint peeling off a wall

black blotches - oozing poisonous black slime that burns on contact. When damaged more slime blotches will appear. Slime can be carefully squeezed out of the blotches by the goblins and used as a means of defence or attack. **AVOID THE GOO !!!!**

INK CAP GOBLIN HABITATS AND WAYS

They live deep in the woods, surrounded by shaggy ink cap mushrooms and other fungi
They like damp conditions
They live in small groups
Food source: unknown

WHEN FIGHTING INK CAP GOBLINS...

Ideally wear protective gloves and overalls
Alternatively, attack from behind so they cannot attack with slime or drop a sack over the goblin's head and then attack
N.B. Remember they are weak and easily hurt but AVOID THE POISON!

Plans of attack with Ink Cap Goblins

Qualities of Goblin Goo:

black

sticky

poisonous

like treacle

How To Defeat Ink Cap Goblins

washing line
water butt
feet and kicking

GOBLIN GOO –
Important fact,
goblin goo makes
goblins' skin
sizzle!!!

Sam the Champion

What did Ug say to the other Ink
Caps Goblins in the cellar?
There isn't mush-room in here!

GERONIMO!
Bring it on!

These are not good
enough notes, Sophie.

Shaggy Ink Cap Fungi compared to Ink Cap Goblins:

Shaggy Ink Caps have a white cap covered with scales. (Ink Cap Goblins have similarly shaped heads and skin that is covered in flakes.)

Shaggy Ink Caps secrete a black ink that drips from gills. (Ink Cap Goblins have goo that drips from the edges of their skin.)

Clumps of Shaggy Ink Caps can be found from spring to autumn **Imagine a clump of Ink Cap Goblins - ew!)**

Shaggy Ink Caps are edible when they are young

Yum! King Ug's ear on toast for tea, anyone?

Sophie that's GROSS!

NOTES

What's next in store for Sophie?

Linda Chapman & Lee Weatherly

Sophie
AND THE
Shadow Woods

The
Swamp
Boggles

Only one girl can save the world...

Turn the page
for a sneak peek...

ophie's toes began to tingle. The feeling surged up through her legs, her body, her arms and into her head. She felt a crazy urge to jump and fight as her Guardian powers kicked in. There *had* to be a shadow creature nearby for her to feel like this!

She set off at a super-fast run. The little cul-de-sac came to a dead end, bordering on to the woods. There was a footpath running alongside the trees, and a small white, fluffy dog with a blue bow perched on its head and a sparkly collar was sniffing around the trail of slime. Sophie skidded to a halt beside it. The trail went straight into the trees. She picked up the pampered-looking little dog and moved it well away from the horrible slime.

"I'm going in!" she called over her shoulder to Sam, who was still running down the cul-de-sac.

"Wait for me!" he called, but Sophie took no notice. She raced into the trees following the trail.

Branches grabbed at her like crooked fingers and thorny brambles caught at her ankles, but Sophie was intent on following the slime. The trees pressed close all around her, and the shadows deepened.

Suddenly she saw something just ahead of her, moving through the gloom. She caught her breath. It was a shadow creature! But it certainly wasn't an Ink Cap Goblin. It had greeny-brown skin, enormous bony hands hanging by its sides, straggly wisps of hair that looked like pondweed and slime dripping from its toes.

The Guardian powers were throbbing through her, making her feel strong and powerful.

"Hey you!" she shouted, speeding up. "Mr Bony Hands!"

The creature swung round. It was a head taller than Sophie, and wore scraps of raggedy clothes. A swampy stench like the smell of rotten eggs billowed towards her.

"You!" it said in a burbling, slimy voice. "The girl who's the new Guardian of the Gateway."

"Yep, that's me," said Sophie, stopping and folding her arms.

For a moment, they both just stared at each other. Suddenly, Sophie became aware of strange rustles in the trees around her, coming from the gloomy shadows. A flicker of fear rose up inside her, but she pushed it down.

"What were you doing out on the street?" she demanded. "Someone saw you!"

"So?" The creature gave a squelchy laugh. Its teeth were very long and sharp, Sophie noticed uneasily.

She tried to sound braver than she felt. "So, stay away from the town and the people in it."

"Ha, you wish! For your information, I have a job to do." The creature opened its slimy fingers. In its palm glinted the large iron key to the gateway.

Sam ran up behind Sophie, panting and out of breath. "It's got the key!" he gasped, propping his hands on his knees.

"How did you get that?" burst out Sophie. "Did you take it from the Ink Caps?"

"Take it? No, they *gave* it to me!" The creature gave a low, wet-sounding chuckle that made Sophie's skin crawl. "We've got a deal. I'm going to use it to find the gem, and then they'll open the gateway."

Sophie stared at the key. If she could just get it back, then it wouldn't matter where the gems were hidden – the shadow creatures wouldn't be able to open the gateway! She lunged forwards, but her opponent was fast. It jerked the key away with a snarl as it swiped at her with long, claw-like fingers.

Sophie jumped back, surprise flashing through her. The Ink Cap Goblins had been cowardly, but this thing didn't seem scared at all! She attacked again, her right foot lashing out in a high kick aimed at its chest. *Ha!* she thought in triumph, waiting for the crunch...

SQUISH!

It was as if her foot had hit a pillow filled with water. The creature's body was so soggy that her kick didn't seem to bother it at all.

Sophie gasped in surprise as her opponent grabbed her foot and yanked upwards, just as Grandpa had done in the training session. "*Oof!*"

She thumped back on to the ground. Before she could spring to her feet, it was looming over her, showing its long, spiny teeth.

"Get off her!" Sam yelled. He threw his lunch box at it. There was a splatting sound as it hit the creature and dropped to the floor.

Through the trees, Sophie heard a very faint cry.

"Cutie-Pie! Cutie! Please come back!"

But she didn't have time to think about it. She felt the creature's hands on her shoulders, saw its pointed teeth coming closer to her face, smelt its rotten breath. She struggled as hard as she could, but her fingers just sank into its squishy skin. Panic rushed through her. How could she fight something that she couldn't hurt or grip or kick?

"No!" she cried as the creature's teeth came closer...

"Do you have what it takes to be the NEXT GUARDIAN?"

Prove your worth for a chance to win AWESOME prizes!
It's simple and fun!

 Read the *Sophie and the Shadow Woods* series
Answer three questions about each book
Pass a stage, collect a gem, enter for great prizes/freebies
Pass SIX stages and get entered into the grand draw!

Stage One

Answer these simple questions about *The Goblin King*:

1. Where was the green gem hidden?
2. What makes Ink Cap Goblin's skin sizzle?
3. Who is the Goblin King?

Got the answers? Go to:
www.sophieandtheshadowwoods.com
and start your journey!

Look out for Stage Two in
The Swamp Boggles, out in June.

Good Luck!